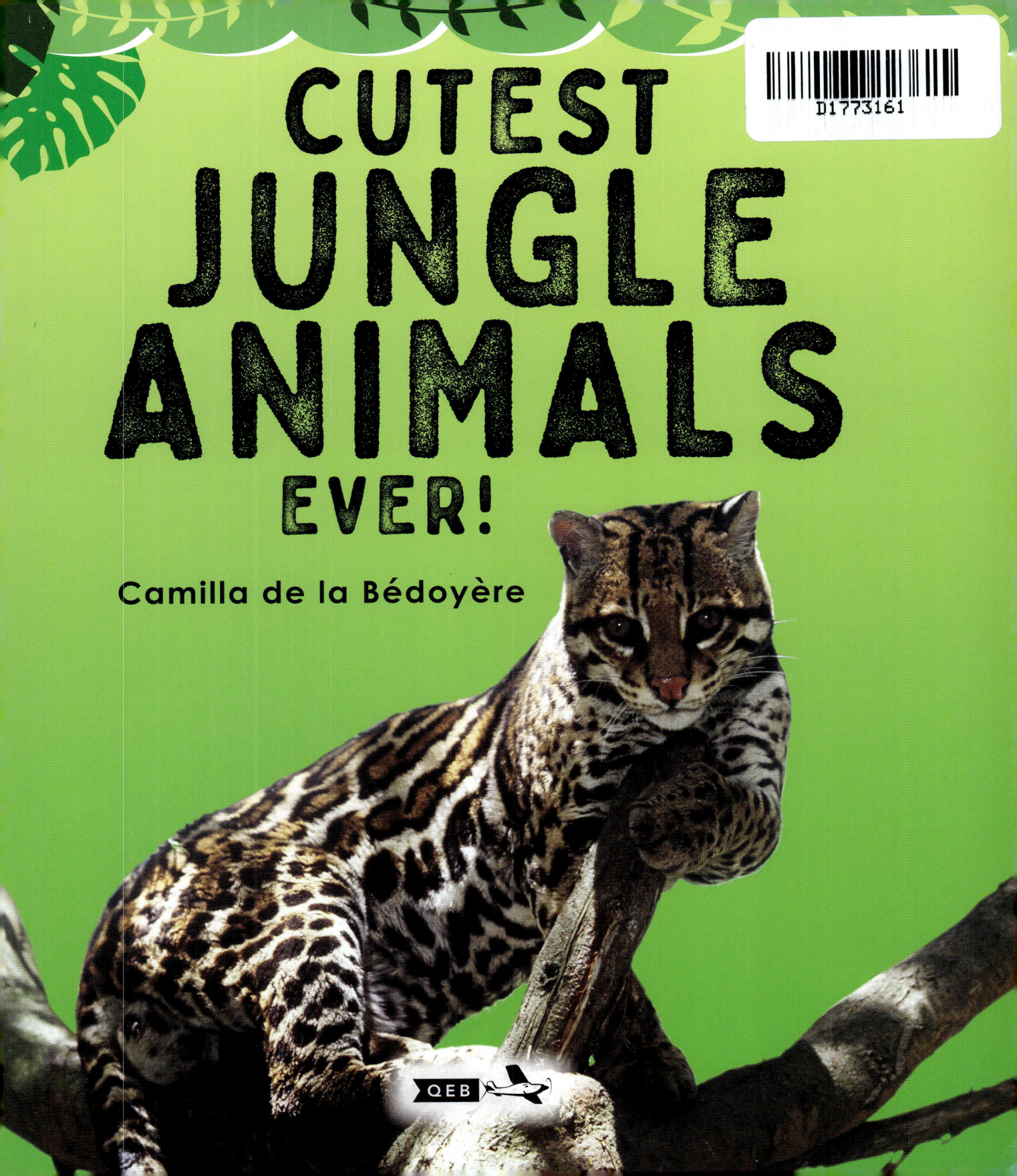

Cutest Jungle Animals Ever!

Camilla de la Bédoyère

Author: Camilla de la Bédoyère
Editor: Emily Pither
Designer: Cloud King Creative
Picture Researcher: Sarah Bell

© 2020 Quarto Publishing plc

First Published in 2020 by QEB Publishing,
an imprint of The Quarto Group.
26391 Crown Valley Parkway,
Suite 220
Mission Viejo, CA 92691, USA
T: +1 949 380 7510
F: +1 949 380 7575
www.QuartoKnows.com

All rights reserved. No part of this publication may be reproduced, stored in a retrieval system, or transmitted in any form or by any means, electronic, mechanical, photocopying, recording, or otherwise, without the prior permission of the publisher, nor be otherwise circulated in any form of binding or cover other than that in which it is published and without a similar condition being imposed on the subsequent purchaser.

A CIP record for this book is available from the Library of Congress.

ISBN 978-0-7112-5333-9

Manufactured in Guangdong, China TT102019

9 8 7 6 5 4 3 2 1

The Jungle Stats contain information about the color, size, cuteness rating and location of each animal.

JUNGLE STATS

Color: Black fur and pale faces

Size: Up to 3 feet tall

Western and central Africa

CONTENTS

Bird of Paradise 4
Black and White Ruffed Lemur 6
Bongo 8
Bonobo 10
Bushbaby 12
Capybara 14
Chameleon 16
Chimpanzee 18
Clouded Leopard 20
Colobus Monkey 22
Cotton-top Tamarin 24
Crowned Pigeon 26
Deer 28
Dhole 30
Eastern Cottontail Rabbit 32
Elephant 34
Giant Anteater 36
Gibbon 38
Golden Lion Tamarin 40
Gorilla 42
Gray Slender Loris 44
Hummingbird 46
Hyacinth Macaw 48
Indian Giant Squirrel 50

Jaguar 52
Kinkajou 54
Leopard 56
Malayan Tapir 58
Ocelot 60
Okapi 62
Orangutan 64
Owl 66
Pangolin 68
Peacock 70
Quokka 72
Ring-tailed Lemur 74
Rufous Bettong 76
Scarlet Ibis 78
Sloth 80
Sloth Bear 82
Squirrel Monkey 84
Striped Possum 86
Tarsier 88
Tiger 90
Toucan 92
Tree Frog 94
Photo credits 96

BIRD OF PARADISE

There are about 40 types of bird of paradise and most of them live on an island called New Guinea.

Male birds of paradise are more colorful than the females. They love to dance and showoff their fine feathers!

JUNGLE STATS

Color: Many different colors

Size: 5 to 40 inches long

Island of New Guinea, Southeast Asia

BLACK AND WHITE RUFFED LEMUR

Lovely lemurs are monkey-like animals with thick fur and a long tail.

Lemurs climb through the trees, carefully picking fruit off the branches. Some lemurs carry their babies with them, but others leave the youngsters in a nest. Ruffed lemurs make loud barking sounds when they see danger.

JUNGLE STATS

Color: Black and white

Size: Up to 4 feet long

Island of Madagascar, near Africa

BONGO

Bongos are shy deer. They have white stripes, big ears, and long horns.

Young bongos are called calves and they live in herds with their moms. When a mom can't see her calf in the thick jungle, she makes a "moo" sound to tell it to come back to her.

JUNGLE STATS

Color: Red-brown with white stripes

Size: 5 to 8 feet long

Rainforests of central and western Africa

BONOBO

Bonobos are adorable apes! They live in African jungles.

A baby bonobo stays with its mom until it is about five years old. She teaches her baby where to find the best jungle plants to eat.

JUNGLE STATS

Color: Black skin and fur, red lips

Size: Up to 3 feet tall

Forests and grasslands in central Africa

BUSHBABY

Bushbabies spend the hot day fast asleep in jungle trees.

At sunset, a bushbaby stirs from its rest and sets off to hunt. It can twist and turn its large ears to listen for bugs, lizards, and birds. It catches them with its tiny hands.

JUNGLE STATS

Color: Brown to gray

Size: Up to 16 inches long

African jungles

CAPYBARA

The charming capybara looks like a giant guineapig!

When the sun is hot these furry animals love to laze in the water and wait until dark before finding plants to eat. Their ears, eyes, and nose are on the top of their heads so they can look for danger even when they are swimming.

JUNGLE STATS

Color: Brown

Size: Up to 4.5 feet long

Near water in South American jungles

CHAMELEON

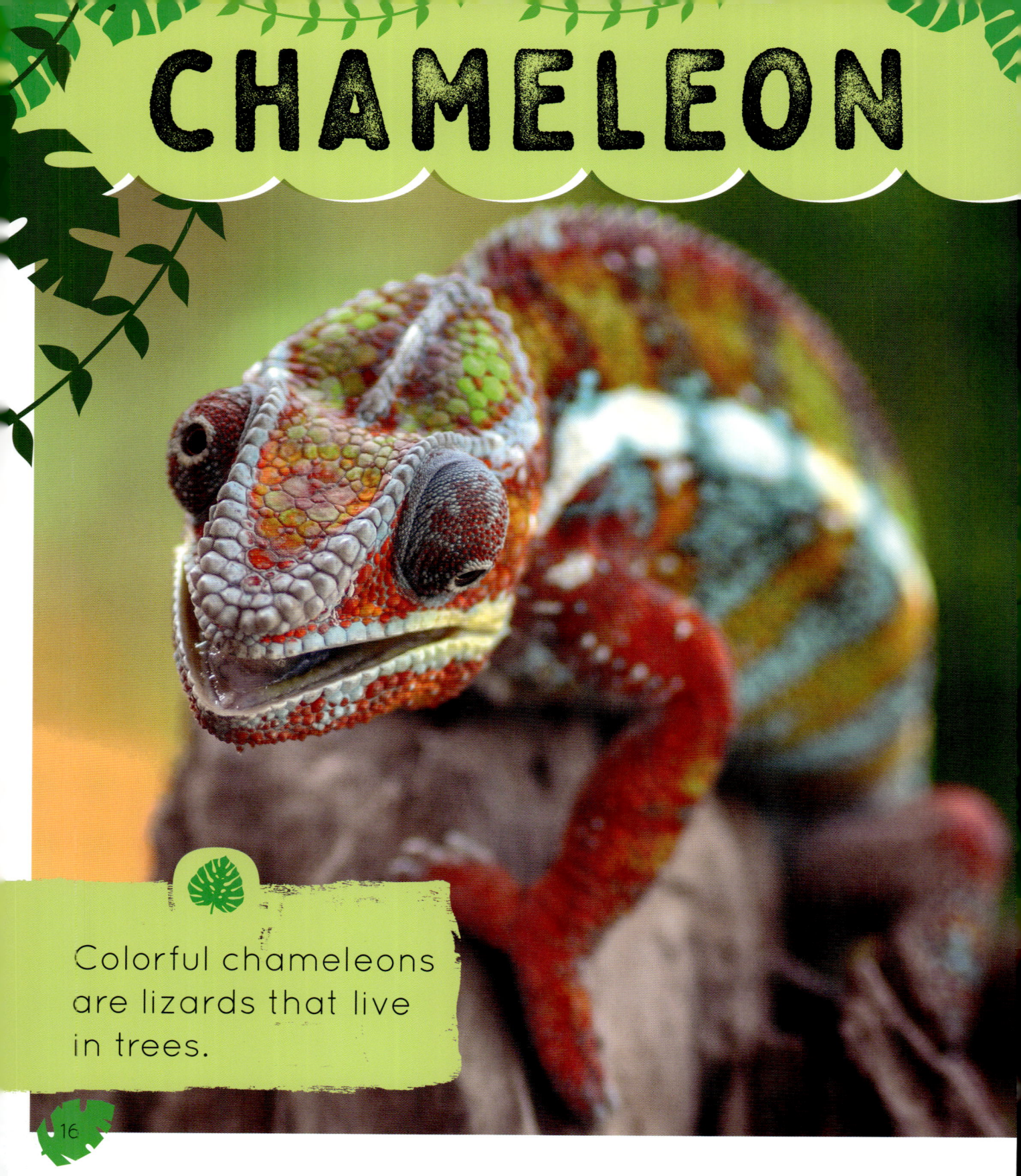

Colorful chameleons are lizards that live in trees.

They can change the color of their scaly skin, and turn beautiful shades of red, pink, green, blue, and yellow. Chameleons have long, sticky tongues that they shoot out of their mouths to catch bugs.

JUNGLE STATS

Color: Many different colors

Size: 3 to 30 inches long

Africa and Madagascar

17

CHIMPANZEE

The jungle is a playground for cheeky chimps. They can run, jump, climb, and roll around on the forest floor!

Chimps are noisy animals and they call out to each other with hoots. Chimps make nests in the trees and sleep there at night.

JUNGLE STATS

Color: Black fur and pale faces

Size: Up to 3 feet tall

Western and central Africa

CLOUDED LEOPARD

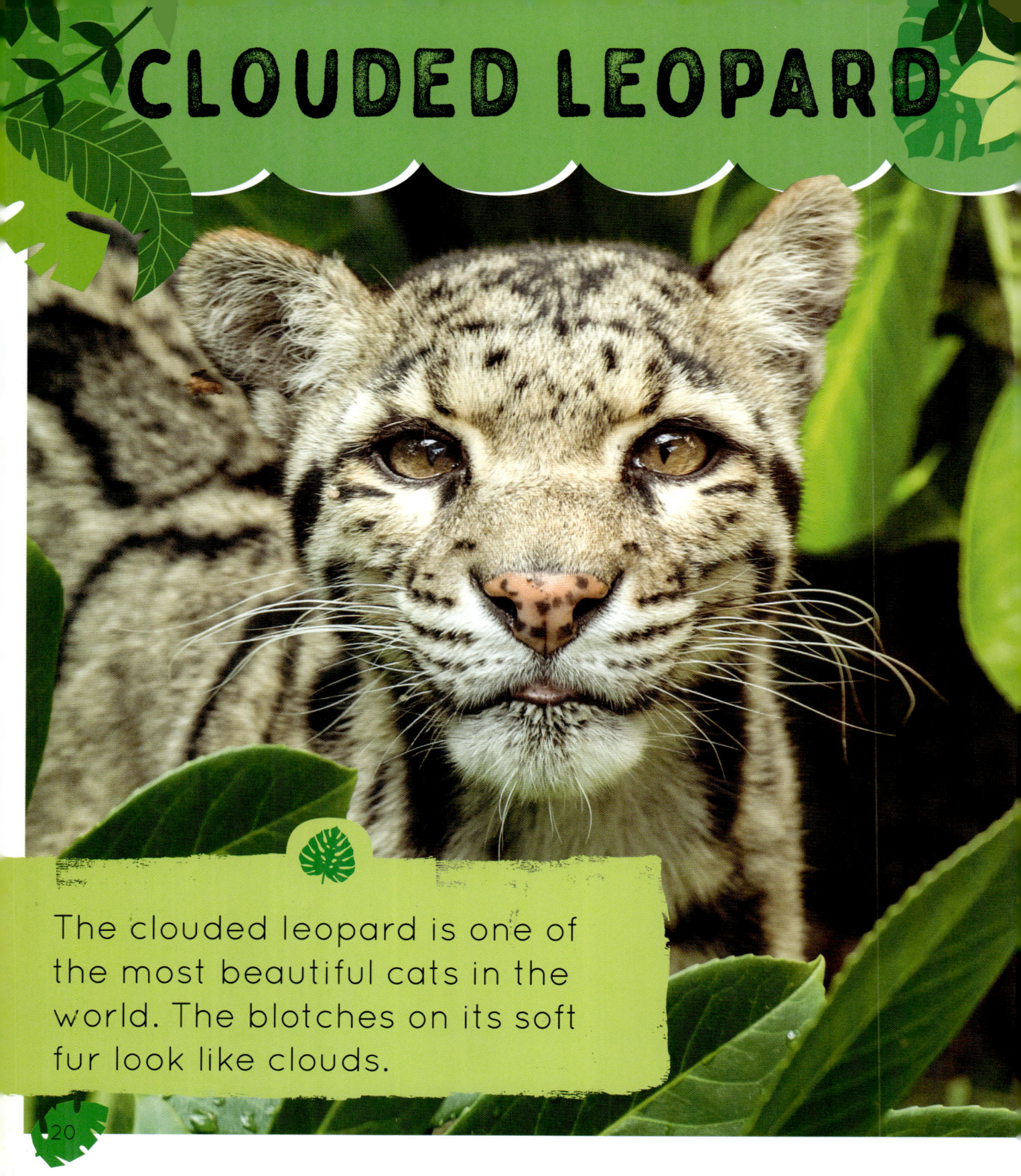

The clouded leopard is one of the most beautiful cats in the world. The blotches on its soft fur look like clouds.

Few people have been lucky enough to see a clouded leopard because these fluffy hunters are very shy and they spend most of their time hiding in trees.

JUNGLE STATS

Color: Cream and reddish fur, with black marks

Size: Up to 3.5 feet long

Southeast Asia

COLOBUS MONKEY

These cute monkeys use their hands to grip onto branches as they swing through the jungle.

Black and white colobus monkeys have long, fluffy tails and can leap more than 26 feet between trees without falling! They eat leaves and fruit.

JUNGLE STATS

Color: Black and white

Size: Up to 2 feet long

Central Africa

COTTON-TOP TAMARIN

The fluffy white fur on a tamarin's head is called a crest or crown.

Cotton-top tamarins live together in big families and they take care of each other. They even use their claws to brush each other's fur to keep it clean and shiny!

JUNGLE STATS

Color: Black and white

Size: 8 to 10 inches long

Colombia, South America

CROWNED PIGEON

This beautiful bird has a crown, or crest, of fluffy feathers and red eyes.

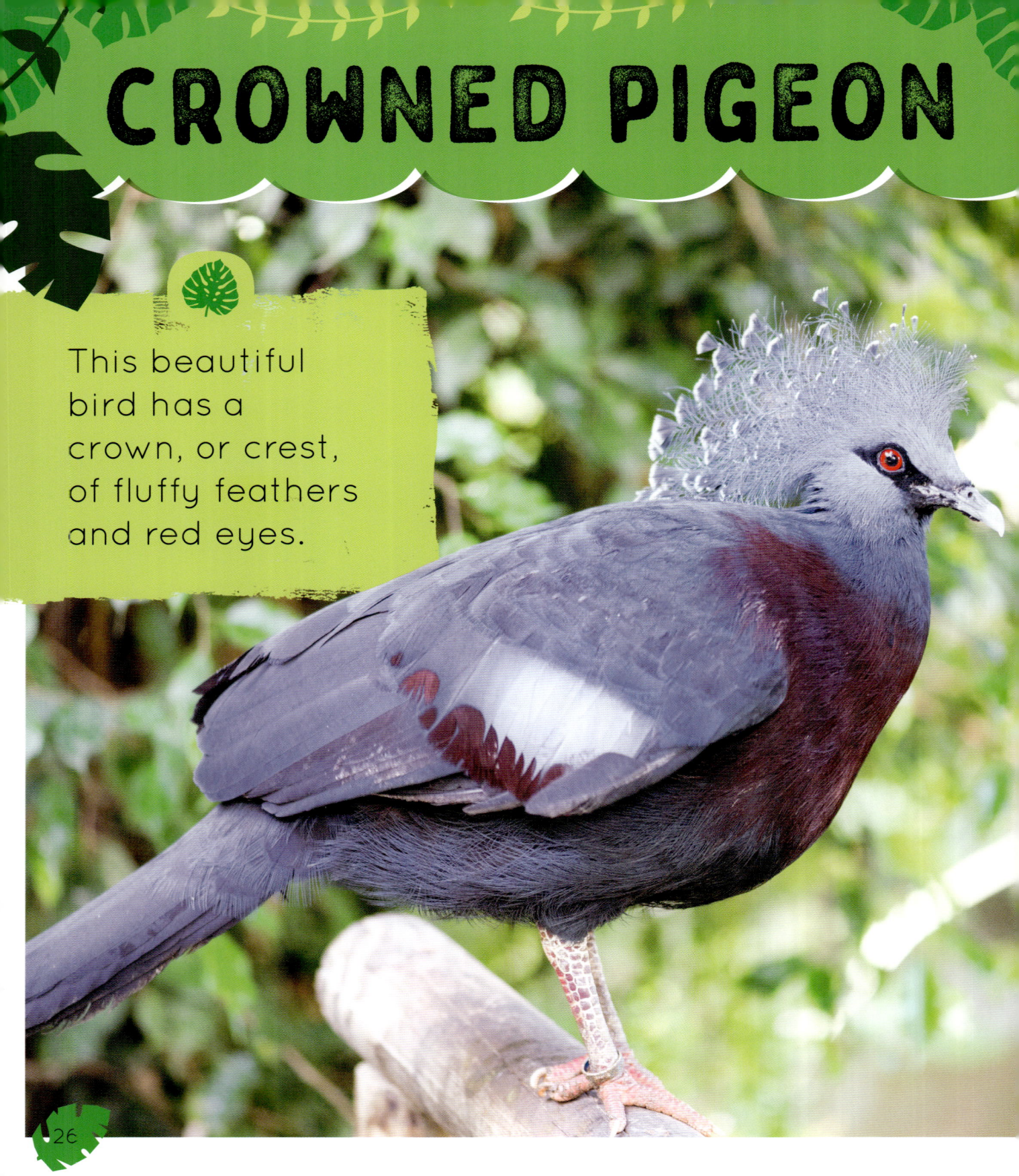

It builds its nest in the jungle and lays just one egg at a time. The chick hatches about four weeks later. Crowned pigeons eat bugs, fruit, and seeds.

JUNGLE STATS

Color: Blue-gray with purple-red parts

Size: Up to 29 inches long

Island of New Guinea, Southeast Asia

DEER

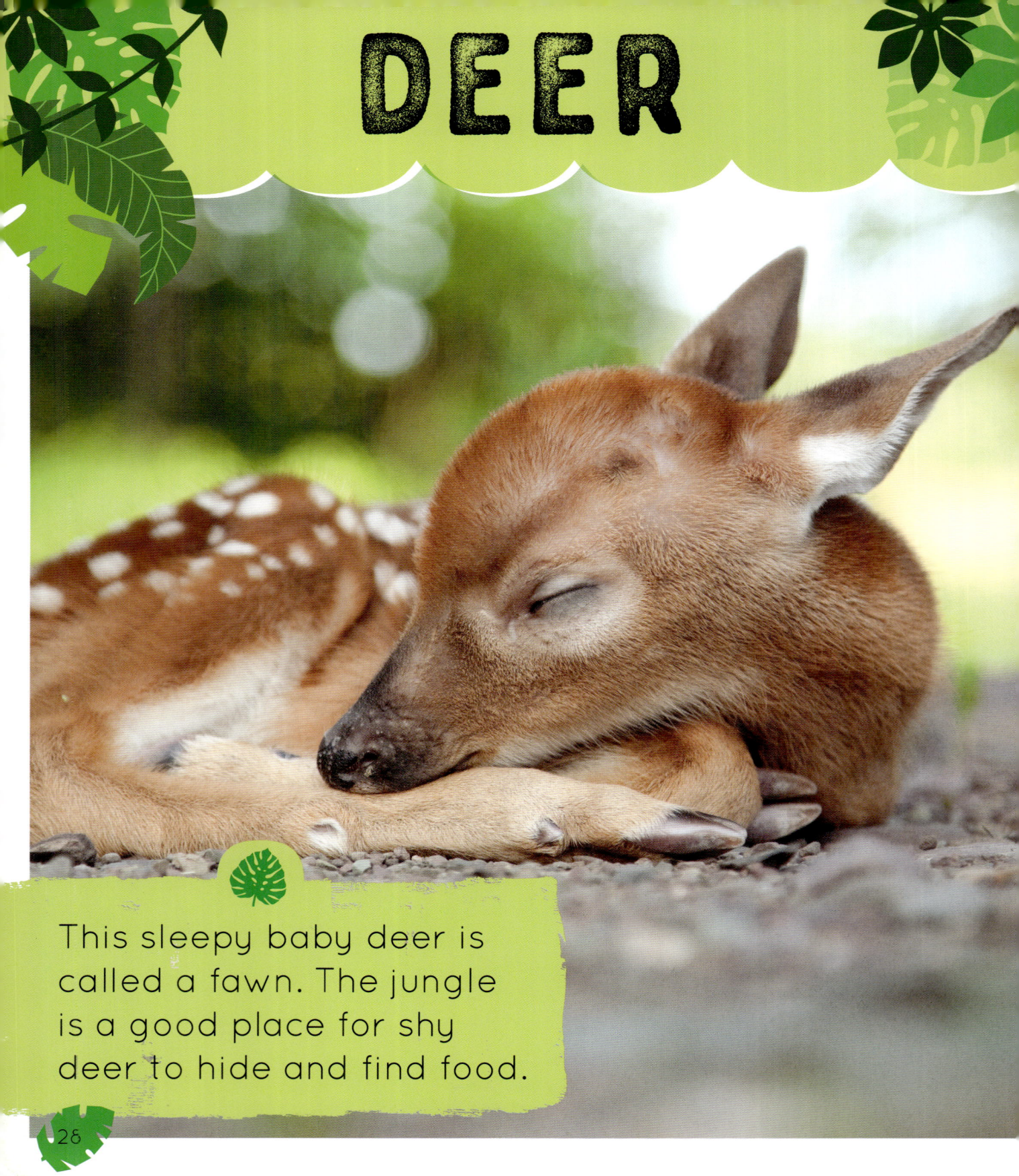

This sleepy baby deer is called a fawn. The jungle is a good place for shy deer to hide and find food.

There are plenty of leaves, flowers, and berries for deer to nibble on. Their spots help them to hide in the dark shadowy places below trees and bushes.

JUNGLE STATS

Color: Red, brown, gray, or fawn

Size: 5 to 8.5 feet long

Southeast Asia, Central, and South America

DHOLE

Dholes are shy, wild dogs that live in Asia. They have red-brown fur and long, bushy tails that they wag, just like pet dogs.

Baby dholes are called pups and they are gray-brown. Dholes are playful animals and they love to jump around in water on a hot day.

JUNGLE STATS

Color: Reddish-brown with cream parts

Size: Up to 18 inches long

Southeast Asia

EASTERN COTTONTAIL RABBIT

Cottontail rabbits have cute, fluffy tails that look like a soft puff of cotton wool.

Rabbits are always on the lookout for danger! They stand on their back feet to look all around and sniff the air. When they are scared, they run fast, zigzagging between plants to find a hiding place.

JUNGLE STATS

Color: Reddish-brown to gray

Size: 15 to 20 inches long

North, Central, and South America

ELEPHANT

Elephants use their trunks to breathe, drink, eat, spray water, and cuddle!

Many elephants live on grasslands, but others live in the jungle. They have long teeth called tusks that they use to move the plants out of their way. A baby elephant is called a calf.

JUNGLE STATS

Color: Gray or brown

Size: Up to 13 feet long

Africa and Southeast Asia

GIANT ANTEATER

An anteater's long nose is called a snout, and it's perfect for sniffing for ants!

Anteaters open ant nests with their claws and lick the ants up with their long, sticky tongue. Baby anteaters cling to mom's back. They watch her hunt ants and learn how to find the best nests.

JUNGLE STATS

Color: Gray, black, and white

Size: Up to 6 feet long

Central and South America

GIBBON

Gibbons are the kings of the swingers! They have very long arms and they use them to hang from trees and swing from branch to branch.

A baby uses its little hands to cling tightly to its mom's fur as she races through the trees.

JUNGLE STATS

Color: Cream, gray, black, or brown

Size: Up to 3 feet tall

Jungles of Southeast Asia

39

GOLDEN LION TAMARIN

These tamarins are famous for their beautiful, silky fur.

Golden lion tamarins are small enough to dart around in the trees, finding lizards, frogs, snails, and bugs to eat. Mom has two babies at a time, and dad helps her take care of them.

JUNGLE STATS

Color: Golden-red

Size: Up to 15 inches long

Jungles of South America

GORILLA

These big, hairy apes live in family groups. The father gorilla looks after his family.

Baby gorillas love to play in the jungle. When they are tired, they sneak back to mom for a kiss and a cuddle.

JUNGLE STATS

Color: Black

Size: 4 to 6 feet tall

Central and western Africa

GRAY SLENDER LORIS

A loris is a quiet animal. It creeps through the trees at night, looking for bugs to eat.

It has big eyes that help it to see in the dark. When mom goes to hunt, she leaves her baby in a tree and other lorises come to babysit!

JUNGLE STATS

Color: Gray with cream fur on belly and face

Size: Up to 11 inches long

India and Sri Lanka

HUMMINGBIRD

A hummingbird darts to a flower. It flaps its wings so fast they make a humming sound.

These small birds hover by a flower and use their long beaks to suck the sugary nectar from inside. They twinkle and glitter in the dark forest, like flying jewels.

JUNGLE STATS

Color: Many different colors

Size: 2 to 10 inches long

The Americas, mainly tropical forests

HYACINTH MACAW

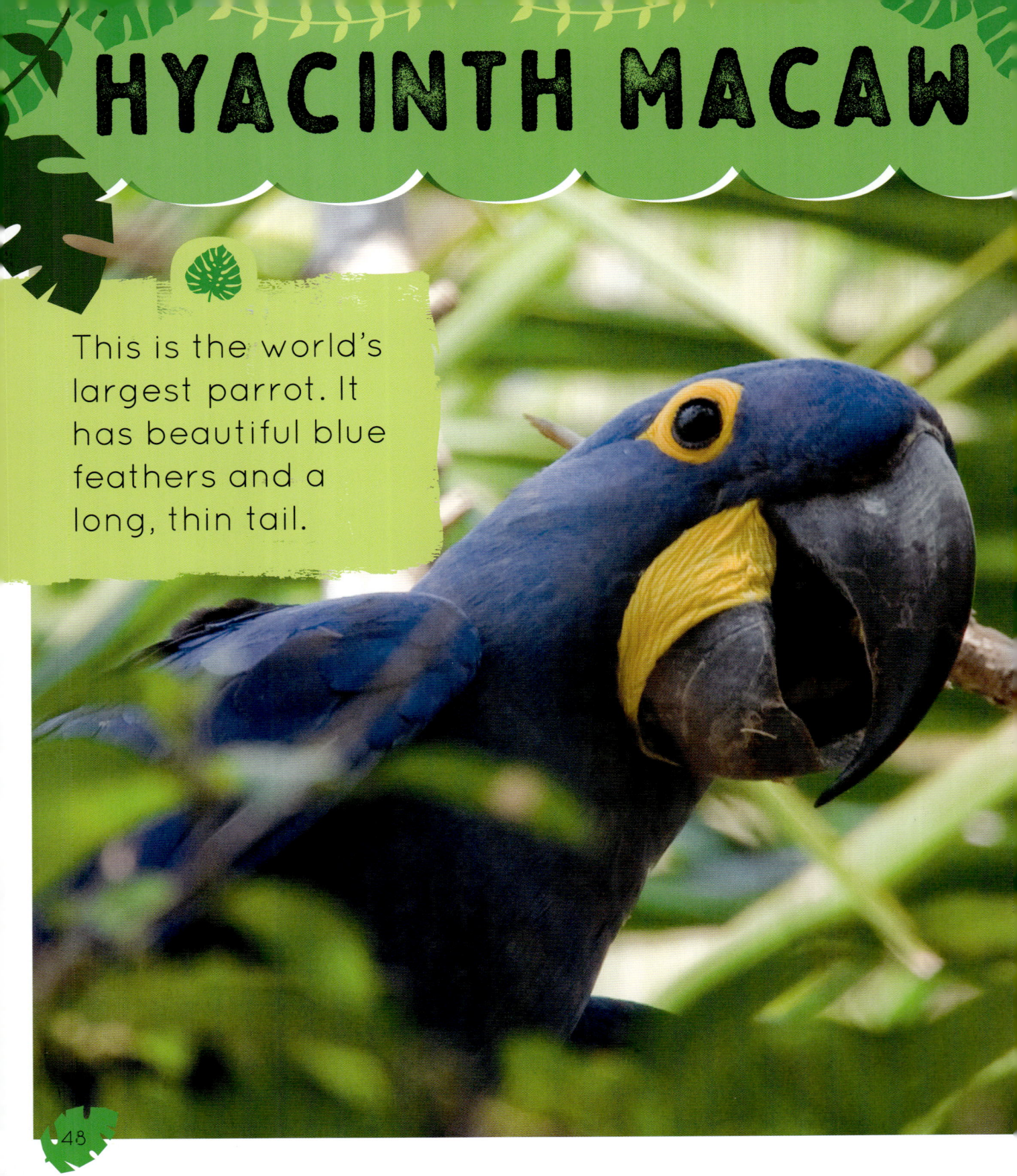

This is the world's largest parrot. It has beautiful blue feathers and a long, thin tail.

Hyacinth macaws hop about between branches or fly to the forest floor to pick up nuts and fruits. They often hang upside down when they use their big, hooked beaks to crack open nuts!

JUNGLE STATS

Color: Blue feathers with golden yellow skin

Size: Up to 40 inches long

Amazon rainforest, South America

INDIAN GIANT SQUIRREL

These colorful squirrels with big, bushy tails are at home in the treetops. They can leap more than 16.4 feet between branches.

Squirrels build nests from leaves and twigs and keep their babies safe there while they grow bigger.

JUNGLE STATS

Color: Dark red to brown with cream patches

Size: 14 to 16 inches long

Forests of India

JAGUAR

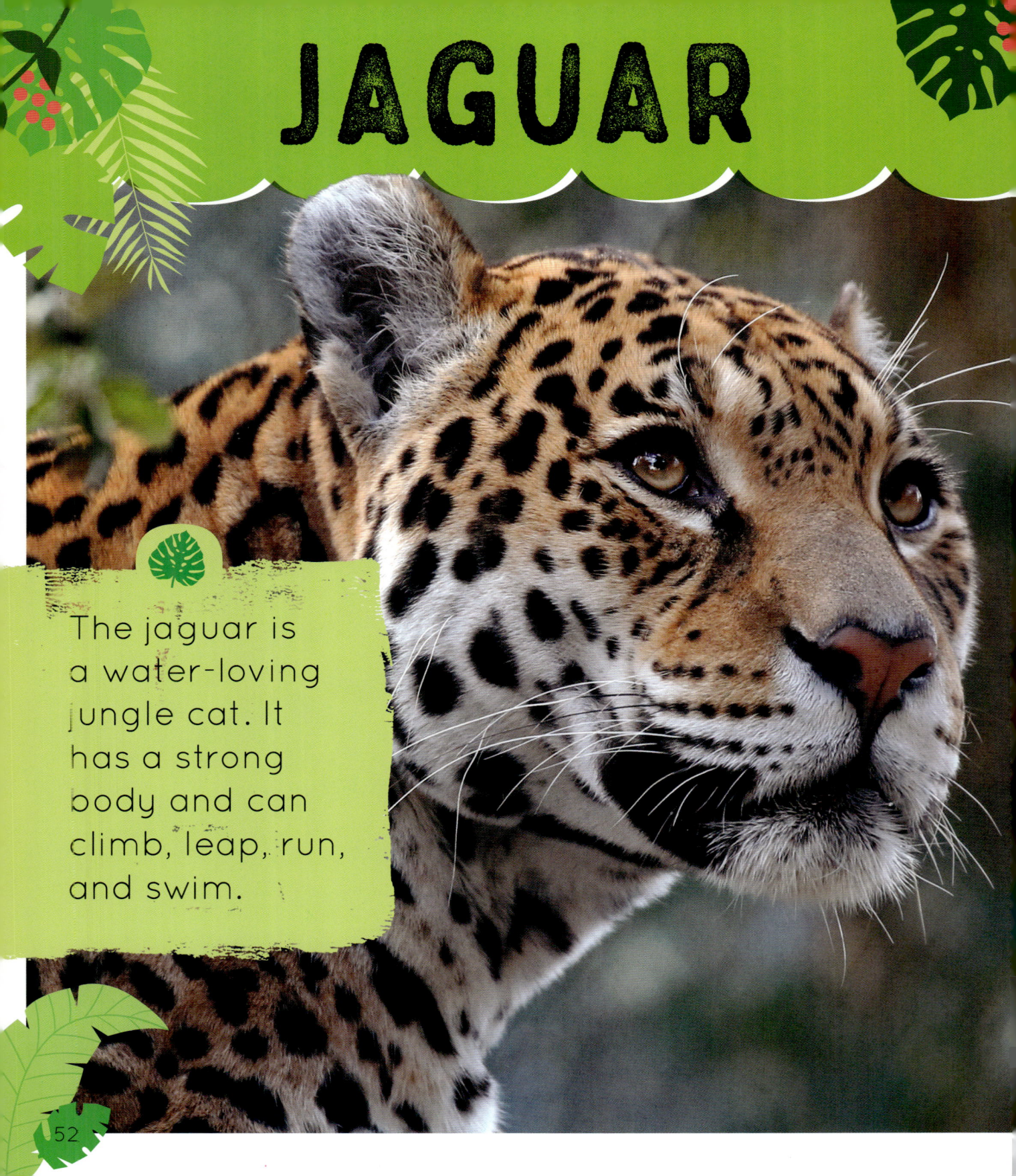

The jaguar is a water-loving jungle cat. It has a strong body and can climb, leap, run, and swim.

It uses its long tail to help it balance when it walks along branches. The spotty marks on a jaguar's fur are called rosettes.

JUNGLE STATS

Color: Fawn, cream, and black

Size: Up to 6 feet long

Central and South America

KINKAJOU

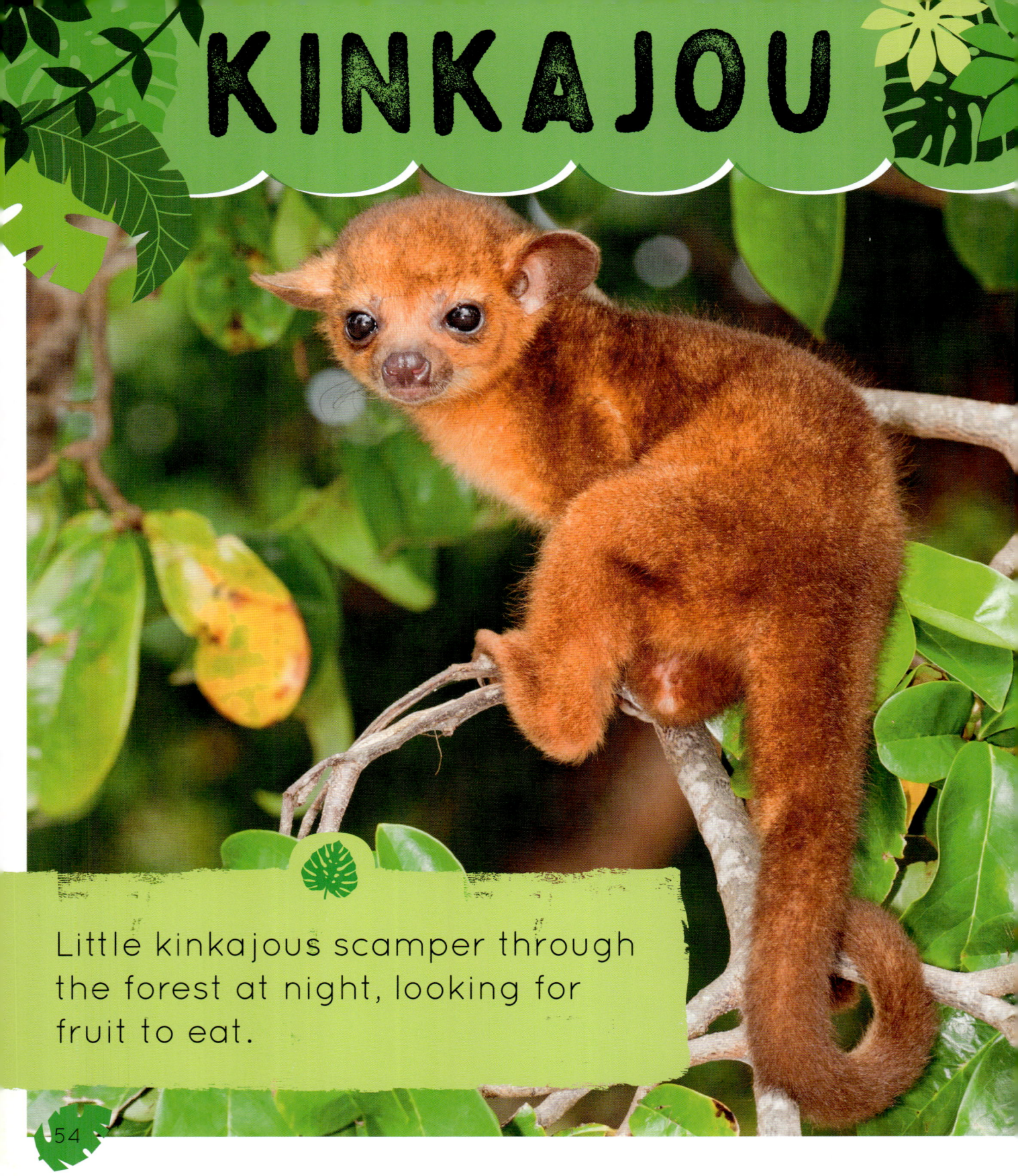

Little kinkajous scamper through the forest at night, looking for fruit to eat.

Kinkajous spend most of their time in the trees. They use their long, bushy tails to hold onto branches while they hang upside down. Baby kinkajous are called pups.

JUNGLE STATS

Color: Golden-red

Size: 15 to 30 inches long

Central and South America

LEOPARD

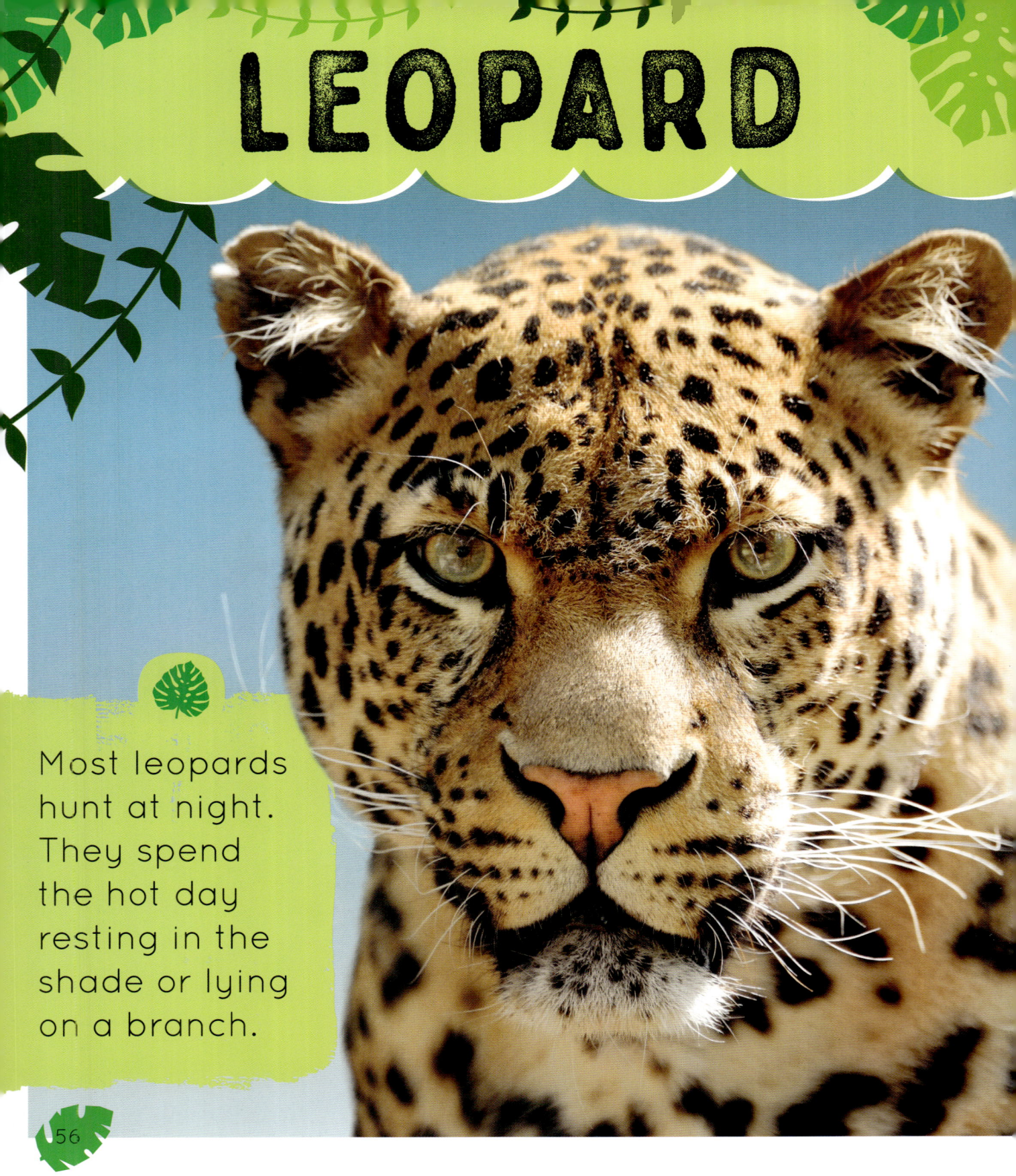

Most leopards hunt at night. They spend the hot day resting in the shade or lying on a branch.

They like to watch other animals move around below the tree. They even hide their food in a tree, so they can eat it later.

JUNGLE STATS

Color: Gold-red with black marks and pale belly

Size: Up to 6 feet long

Africa and Asia

MALAYAN TAPIR

Tapirs look like pigs with long noses.

They scamper quickly through the forest, sniffing at the ground and listening for jaguars and other hunters. Baby tapirs have colors and patterns that help them to hide in the shadows.

JUNGLE STATS

Color: Black and white

Size: 6 to 8 feet long

Southeast Asia

OCELOT

Ocelots love to sit in the treetops and watch the world go by.

When the sun sets, ocelots climb down from the trees and prowl through the dark forest, looking for small animals to hunt. These cats can purr, but they cannot roar.

JUNGLE STATS

Color: Red-gold and cream with black marks

Size: Up to 39 inches long

North, Central, and South America

OKAPI

An okapi is also called a forest zebra because it has striking stripes.

Okapis have very long tongues that they use to curl around leaves and rip them off a tree. When two okapis meet in the jungle, they make "chuff" sounds to say "hi".

JUNGLE STATS

Color: Brown-black with white stripes, cheeks, and legs

Size: 6 to 7 feet long

Central Africa

ORANGUTAN

Orangutans are big apes that live in the rainforests of Asia.

They love to climb trees and eat the juicy fruits that grow in the forest. Their favorite is the durian fruit, which smells like stinky socks!

JUNGLE STATS

Color: Red-orange

Size: Up to 4.5 feet tall

Borneo and Sumatra in Southeast Asia

OWL

Owls sleep in tree holes during the day, but at night they swoop silently through the trees.

An owl has huge eyes that help it to see in the dark. It can hear even the smallest sound of a tiny mouse moving on the ground. Baby owls are called owlets.

JUNGLE STATS

Color: Brown, black, tawny, cream

Size: 6 to 21 inches tall

Jungles across the world

PANGOLIN

Pangolins are peculiar little animals with scales on their skin.

When a pangolin is scared it can roll up into a ball. Its scales work like a suit of armor to keep it safe. Pangolins dig up ant and termite nests to reach the bugs inside and lick them up with long tongues.

JUNGLE STATS

Color: Gray, brown, or yellow-brown

Size: Up to 4.5 feet long

Africa and Asia

PEACOCK

The peacock is a stunning bird that lives in dry forests and rainforests.

Peacocks have amazing tail feathers. They spread out their feathers like a fan and shake them when a female, or peahen, is nearby. They sleep in the trees at night.

JUNGLE STATS

Color: Blue and green

Size: Up to 7 feet long

India

QUOKKA

This adorable animal lives in Australia and is known as the happiest animal on the planet.

The baby is called a joey and it is tiny when it is born. The joey stays in the pouch until it is about six months old. Quokkas eat plants and like to live near rivers.

JUNGLE STATS

Color: Sandy-gray with red-brown parts

Size: Up to 22 inches long

Two islands near Australia

RING-TAILED LEMUR

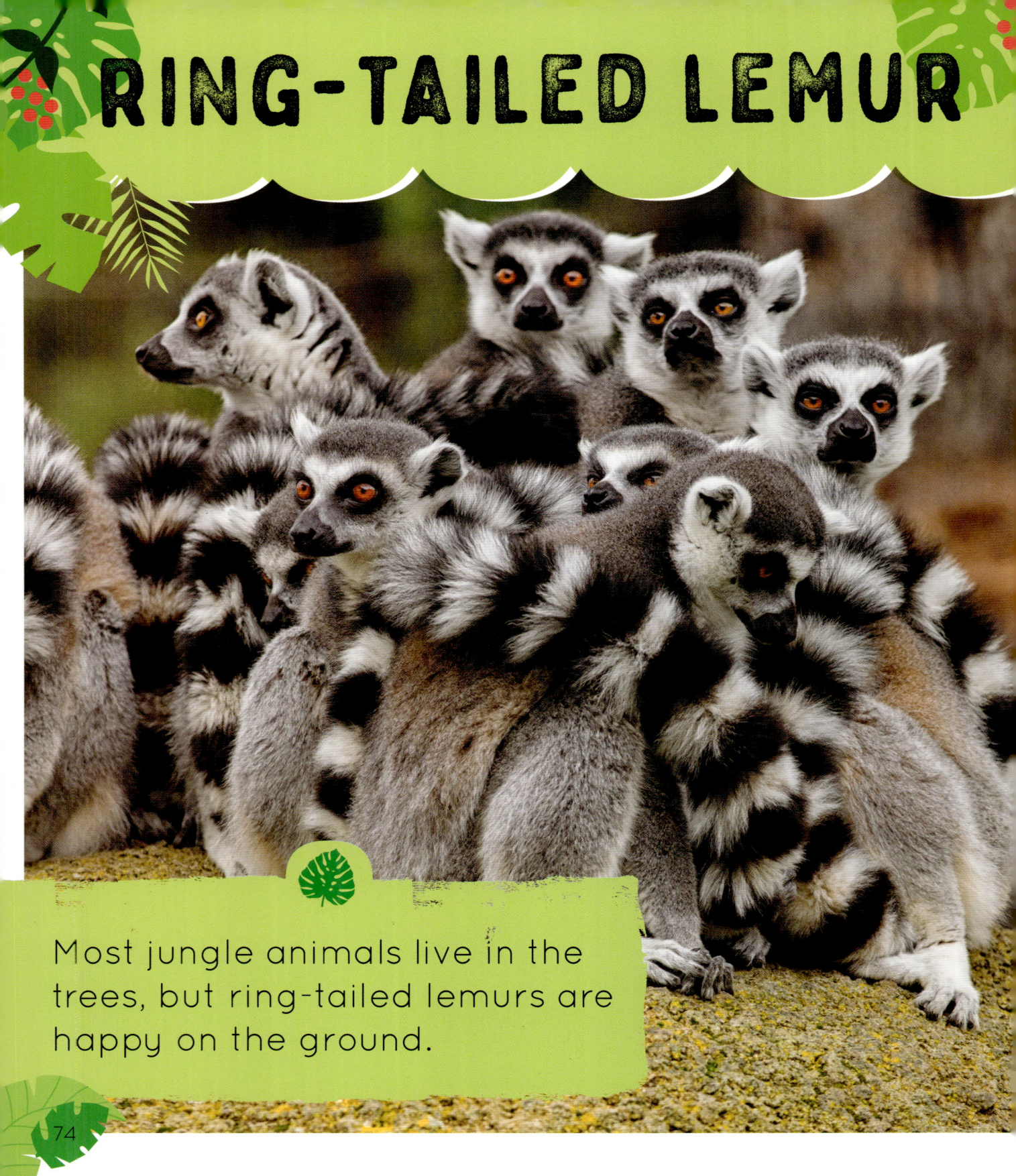

Most jungle animals live in the trees, but ring-tailed lemurs are happy on the ground.

When they run around, they hold their stripy tails up in the air. They live in big family groups and wave their tails to say "hello" to each other.

JUNGLE STATS

Color: Gray, black, and white

Size: Up to 18 inches long

Island of Madagascar

RUFOUS BETTONG

This cuddly little animal hops like a mini-kangaroo!

It has a long, bendy tail that it uses to grab bunches of grass. It uses the grass to make a nest on the dry forest floor, where it sleeps in the day. Rufous bettongs keep their babies in a pouch.

JUNGLE STATS

Color: Red-brown and gray

Size: Up to 21 inches long

Forests of Australia

SCARLET IBIS

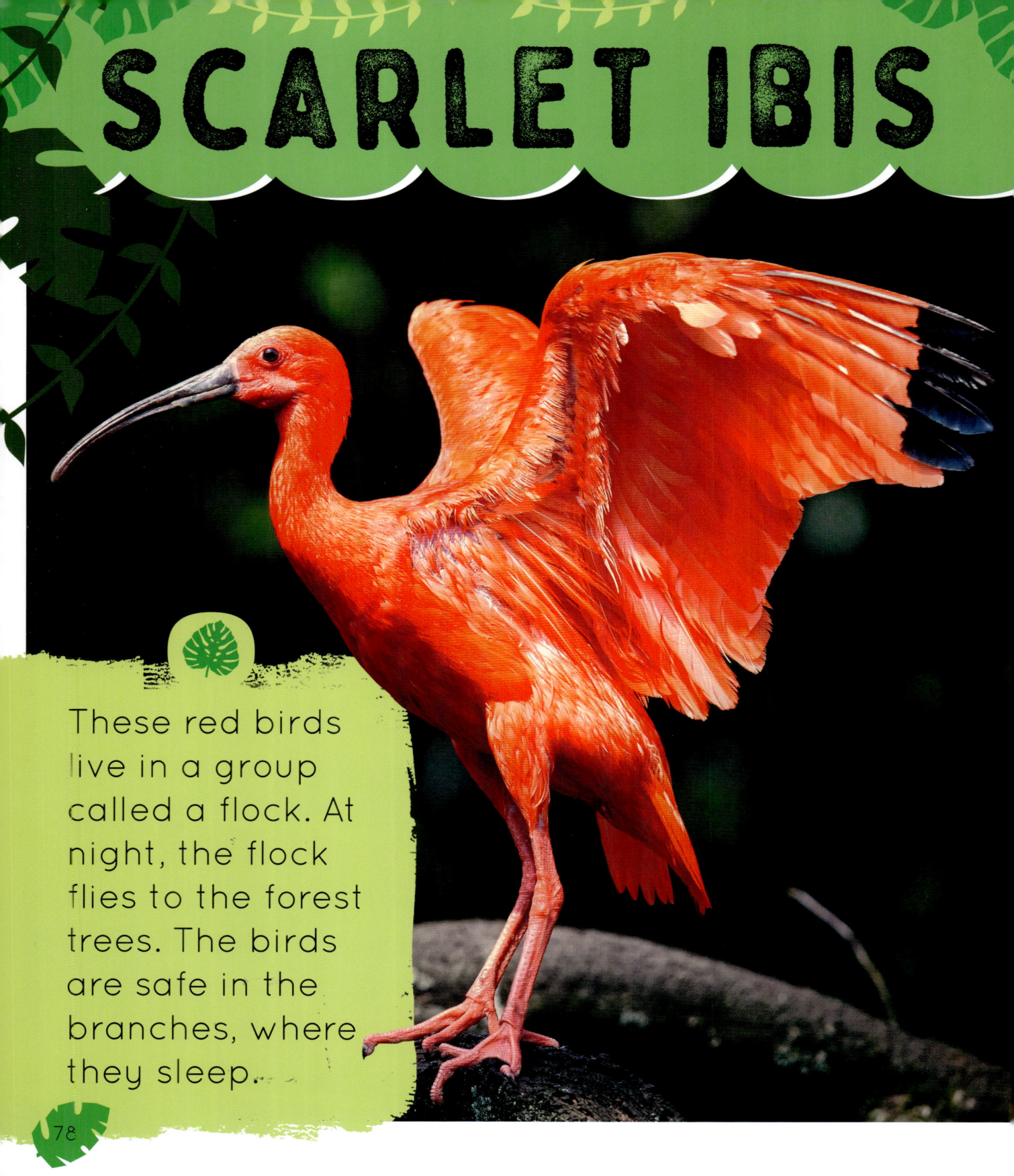

These red birds live in a group called a flock. At night, the flock flies to the forest trees. The birds are safe in the branches, where they sleep.

The scarlet ibis finds food in a river. They use their long, thin beaks to dig crabs and insects out of the soft mud.

JUNGLE STATS

Color: Scarlet-red

Size: 22 to 27 inches long

Central and South America

SLOTH

It's hard to see a sleepy sloth in a tree. Its furry coat has tiny plants living in it, so it looks green, just like the leaves high in the treetops.

Sloths have long, curved claws that they use to hang upside-down.

JUNGLE STATS

Color: Dark brown, red-brown, gray

Size: 18 to 35 inches long

Central and South America

SLOTH BEAR

A sloth bear's thick fur coat is black and shaggy.

These bears walk slowly through the forest, digging up termite nests and sucking up the little bugs. Sloth bears climb trees and hang upside down from the branches!

JUNGLE STATS

Color: Black

Size: 4 to 6 feet long

Southeast Asia

SQUIRREL MONKEY

This little animal can leap and race through the treetops at top speeds, just like a squirrel!

A squirrel monkey's family can have more than 100 monkeys in it. They look for food in the daytime, and huddle together to keep warm and dry when it rains.

JUNGLE STATS

Color: Gray with reddish, white, and black parts

Size: 10 to 14 inches long

South America

STRIPED POSSUM

A striped possum makes its home inside a hole in a tree, where it can hide from hungry snakes.

It sleeps in its den in the day, and at night it climbs through the jungle looking for bugs to eat. Striped possums are good climbers and can reach the highest treetops.

JUNGLE STATS

Color: Black and white

Size: Up to 11 inches long

Australia and New Guinea

TARSIER

A tarsier may be small, but it's a fast and nimble hunter.

It has big eyes and a long tail with a cute tuft of fur on the tip. Tarsiers hold tight onto a tree and then leap. They jump between trees to grab insects, bats, and birds.

JUNGLE STATS

Color: Reddish-brown

Size: 4 to 6 inches long

Southeast Asia

TIGER

A tiger's stripes help it to hide in the jungle shadows and in the long grass by a riverbank.

When the jungle gets too hot, tigers wallow in the water and cool down. Young tigers are called cubs.

JUNGLE STATS

Color: Red-gold and cream with black stripes

Size: Up to 9 feet long

South and East Asia

TOUCAN

Most birds cannot reach the fruit that grows at the tip of a thin branch, but a toucan can!

A toucan stands on a branch and reaches for the fruit with its long beak. Toucans are not good at flying, so they hop between branches.

JUNGLE STATS

Color: Black body with colorful beaks, faces, and chests

Size: Up to 2 feet long

Amazon rainforest, South America

TREE FROG

Tiny tree frogs love the rain, so they are very happy in a rainforest! They lay their eggs in any wet place they find.

Little swimming tadpoles hatch from the eggs and grow into frogs. Tree frogs have special sticky round pads on the tips of their toes for climbing trees.

JUNGLE STATS

Color: Green with white or yellow belly

Size: 1 to 6 inches long

Jungles all over the world

PHOTO CREDITS

Adalbert Dragon/Shutterstock.com 53 centre; Aflo/naturepl.com 63, 67; AkosHorvath/Shutterstock.com 93 right; Alex Hyde/naturepl.com 17 right; Alphotographic/iStock 9; ANDREY GUDKOV/Alamy Stock Photo 11; Ann & Steve; Toon/Robert Harding 35; antonyusbunjamin/Getty Images 16; Anup Shah/naturepl.com 11 left; Arco Images GmbH / Alamy Stock Photo 15, 41 centre; Ariadne Van Zandbergen / Alamy Stock Photo 45; Arnau ramos Oviedo / 500px/Getty Images 27, 27 centre; Avalon/Photoshot License / Alamy Stock Photo 77 right; Axel Gomille/naturepl.com 82; Ben Cranke/naturepl.com 49 centre; Bill Losh/Getty Images 91; BirdImages/iStock 87; borchee/iStock 70; Buiten-Beeld / Alamy Stock Photo; Buiten-Beeld / Alamy Stock Photo 54, 55; chandan kumar v m/Shutterstock.com 54 left; Christian Hutter/imageBROKER/Robert Harding 85 centre; Christian Musat / Alamy Stock Photo 59; Claude Thouvenin/Robert Harding 63 centre; Colin Barrows/Getty Images 85; Colin Langford/Getty Images 20; Conservationist/Shutterstock.com 44; Craig Ingram / Alamy Stock Photo 76; CTK / Alamy Stock Photo 23 centre; Cyril Ruoso/naturepl.com 75; Dan-Edwards/iStock 9 left; dangdumrong/Shutterstock.com 84; Daniel Hernanz Ramos/Getty Images 74; DARKROOM/Balan Madhavan / Alamy Stock Photo 50; David & Micha Sheldon/Getty Images 59 centre; Denis-Huot/naturepl.com 57; Digital Zoo/Getty Images 17; DLILLC/Corbis/VCG 12 left; Edwin Butter/Getty Images 34, 38, 52; Eric Gevaert / Alamy Stock Photo 40, 41; Erika Kirkpatrick/Shutterstock.com 49; Fiona Rogers/naturepl.com 10, 18, 22; Frans Lanting/Robert Harding 37 centre, 89 centre; Freder/Getty Images 56; Gavin Morrison/Shutterstock.com 43 centre; Ger Bosma/Getty Images 39; GERRY ELLIS/ MINDEN PICTURES 90; Getty images: Westend61/Getty Images 37; Henner Damke/Shutterstock.com 64; Hira Punjabi/Getty Images 83 centre; Hoberman Collection / Getty Images 80; Ian Bickerstaff/Getty Images 19 left; Ijdema/Getty Images 30; Iryna Art/Shutterstock.com 6; IVAN LIEMAN / Stringer/Getty Images 42; Jan Vermeer/ Minden Pictures 61; Janette Hill/Robert Harding 73; jeep2499/Shutterstock.com 65; Jiri Hrebicek/Shutterstock.com 62; Jiri Lochman/naturepl.com 77; KAREN BLEIER /Getty Images 37; © Kevin Schafer/age fotostock/Robert Harding 81; Kevin Schafer/naturepl.com 71 left, 73 centre; Kim Sullivan/Robert Harding 91 centre; Konrad Wothe/Robert Harding 47; Kurit afshen/Shutterstock.com 86; Larry Keller, Lititz Pa./Getty Images 46; Londolozi Images/Robert Harding 57 centre; lukaszemanphoto/Shutterstock.com 65 centre; © Mark Boulton 20 / ardea.com 23; Mark Sheridan-Johnson/Shutterstock.com 12; Mark_Kostich/Shutterstock.com 81 centre; Martin Leber / 500px/Getty Images 25 left; Martin Mecnarowski/Shutterstock.com 78; Martin Willis/Shutterstock.com 87 right; © Mary Clay / ardea.com 21 left; Mathew Levine/Shutterstock.com 66; MaZiKab/iStock 58; Melissa Groo/National Geographic Collection 36; MikeLane45/iStock 8; Nicolas Reusens/Getty Images 95; Nigel Hicks / Alamy Stock Photo 24; Oliver Neumann / EyeEm/Getty Images 72; Ondrej Prosicky/Shutterstock.com 92; Panther Media GmbH / Alamy Stock Photo 26; Paul Souders/Getty Images 43; pchoui/Getty Images 94; Per-Andre Hoffmann/Robert Harding 89; Pete Oxford/naturepl.com, 1, 60; Piper Mackay/naturepl.com 93; Ralph Paprzycki / Alamy Stock Photo 48; Raymond Hennessy / Alamy Stock Photo 32; Robert Thompson/naturepl.com 95 left; Robert Harding Picture Library/National Geographic Creative 71; Roland Seitre/naturepl.com 57, 69, 69 centre; Ronald Wittek/age fotostock/Robert Harding 29; Ryan Ladbrook / Alamy Stock Photo 61 centre; Sandesh Kadur/naturepl.com 51; Sergey Taran / Alamy Stock Photo 45 centre; Simia Attentive/Shutterstock.com 39 left; Stan Osolinski/Getty Images 2, 19, 32 left; Stanislav Duben/Shutterstock.com 25; Stefan Cruysberghs/Getty Images 13; Suzi Eszterhas/naturepl.com 7; Sylvain Cordier/Getty Images 21, 83; Sylvain Cordier/natureple.com 79; Talvinder Chohan / Alamy Stock Photo 31 right; tarake/Shutterstock.com 15 left; TeeJe/Getty Images 5; Terryfic3D/Getty Imges 28; Thomas Foldes/Shutterstock.com 14; Tim Graham/naturepl.com 29 left; Tim Laman/Nat Geo Image Collection 5 right; Tim Laman/Nat Geo Image Collection/naturepl.com 4; tratong/Shutterstock.com 75 centre; Ttphoto/Shutterstock.com 35 left; Tuul & Bruno Morandi/Getty Images 88; Val Duncan/Kenebec Images / Alamy Stock Photo 7 centre; Voodison328/Shutterstock.com 67 right; Wang LiQiang/Shutterstock.com 79 right; Winfried Schafer/Robert Harding 47 centre; Yashpal Rathore/naturepl.com 68; Zoonar GmbH / Alamy Stock Photo 33; ZSSD/naturepl.com 31; Zuzana L/Shutterstock.com 71